THE ROSES MINI SAGAS

2022

EDITED

BY

GEORGIA ROSE & SALLY-ROSE RUNHAM

Published by

ISBN 978-1-999357474 (paperback)

British Library Cataloguing in Publication Data

A CIP catalogue record for this book is available from the British Library

Cover design by Simon Emery

What is a Mini Saga?

A mini saga is a fun way to tell a story in 50 words exactly, with a title of no more than 16 words.

It should have a beginning, a middle and an end, and some period of time should pass through the story.

It should have gravity. That's to say, it should make a point which has some drama or psychological truth. It must aim, in fact, to be a saga in miniature.

Foreword

A competition was set up in December 2021 seeking entries for the third Roses Mini Saga competition, deadline of 28th February 2022. The competition was open to everyone, and is of a recognized standard.

The entries are reproduced here, with the winning four entries first and then the other entries included by theme.

The editors would like to thank the authors for the high standard of succinct storytelling.

Index of Mini Sagas

THE ROSES MINI SAGAS

2022

WINNING ENTRIES

The Winning Entry in the 2022 Roses Mini Saga Competition

Conjuring

She danced along the edges of my mind, delicate and fragile, whispering that she wasn't dead. Not really.

I was the one who could bring her back.

She cried, pleaded, begged... Drove me nearly insane. I sighed, grabbed a red pen, and scratched out the death scene in chapter twelve.

Sarah Brentyn

Second Prize in the 2022 Roses Mini Saga Competition

The Flower

She opened her petals in the warming sunshine. Confidently expecting her perfume to attract the insects.

They would bring pollen as they had done for countless generations.

She waited in vain for them to come.

They never came.

There were no insects.

The following year there were no flowers either.

Sonia Kurta

Third Prize in the 2022 Roses Mini Saga Competition

Happy

The lamp was grubby, so I rubbed it hard.
A genie appeared and boomed, "I'll grant you one wish."
"I want to be happy," I asked with a grin.
With a flash of light, I was living in a forest with six dwarves and working down a mine.
Not Happy.

Graham Welton

Highly Commended in the 2022 Roses Mini Saga Competition

I Should Have Stayed at Home

I didn't want to go, but Cathy dragged me.
Backstage I met the singer; we fell in love.
Five years on, he wanted groupies, not the children and me.
Twenty years later, his time has passed.
I'm married to a fat, depressed, ranting alcoholic.
Cathy has much to answer for.

Terry Tyler

THE ROSES MINI SAGAS

2022

ALL OTHER ENTRIES

and previous year's winners

IN THEMES

STOP THE WORLD…

I Dream of Broken Promises. Wake Me, But Not with A Kiss

It was the future: there was fire and brimstone.
It was the past: there was a flood of biblical proportions.
Men killed and raped to make themselves feel better.
To distract us, the democratically elected leader put on a clown costume, and juggled with Latin verbs while riding a trike.

Debbie Collison

Daily Grind

Like yours, my world is round. I circumnavigate it with ease. Keep me company?

Here's the plant, whose leaves sway incessantly. Here's the treasure chest, whose lid opens and closes with monotonous regularity. Here's the log, prostrate on the gravel. Here's the plant again.

It's dead boring, being a goldfish.

Felicity Radcliffe

Climate Summit

She climbed the pinnacle, admired the view, and considered his marriage proposal.

Should she accept – or not? She couldn't envisage their future. She prayed for a crystal ball.

Black clouds appeared, thunder roared, and a boiling sea replaced the verdant fields below.

Clearly her quandary was irrelevant. Time to re-prioritise.

Felicity Radcliffe

Cursing Ferrets

Andrea accidentally saw some videos documenting the brutal live skin-peeling process. She then understood her fur coat was made exactly that way. As an animal lover, she was determined to destroy that bloody business, with her friends in mercenary. After plenty of coincidences during their adventure, they finally made it.

Richard Green

Suffocation

Before, from infection and disease, we died.
Medical science turned that tide.
Now we have a population boom,
We really have too little room.
Eat less,
heat less,
make fewer things,
and the complications all that brings.
Now we reap as we have sewn,
science and nature, our future unknown.

Elizabeth Chandler

Book Launch

"Unbelievable! Tommy Pump from Diesel Street has just self-published the most boring book ever entitled 'The Thoughts of a Spark Plug' and the whole village is queuing to buy a copy from him."

"Yeah!" I replied. "He put up a sign with the words 'Please do not panic buy'."

David Seaton

Eamonn To That

God had blessed Eamonn's mother with a large family.

He was the youngest of nine noisy and hyperactive children.

When he was born, his exhausted mother told his virile father that enough was enough.

She insisted on calling her new son Eamonn because his name sounded like and meant

Amen!

John Sissons

SIMPLE PLEASURES

A Life Less Orderly

Fidelity was an inappropriately named wild child (although she did like to get high).
Marriages, affairs and other mayhems scattered emotional flotsam and jetsam in her wake.
Even in her elder years, when time caught up with her liver and finally slowed her down, she took her Shirley Temple 'dirty'.

Bob Janes

Broken Heating System

Mild October vanished as bitter winter came
        on the day our brand-new air pump failed.
No heat, no help, our body warmth fast draining,
        applying multi-layered clothes, resisting life
expiring.
Then finally on the thirtieth day an engineer we greet.
We sigh and fresh appreciate the bliss of toasty feet!

Meg Brittain Clarke

Finding The Perfect Americano

For years, the beautiful girl with sparkling hazel eyes served me a perfect Americano and made my heart sing.
The café closed down.
For months, I deeply regretted my mumbled "hellos" and shy smiles.
A new café opened.
My heart sang when those familiar hazel eyes shone in my direction.

Wendy Janes

Poo's Stick

The two friends leaned over the bridge.
'Ready, steady, throw!' shouted Robin.
'Ouch!' Screamed Poo.
They raced to the other side.
'Look, mine's the winner,' said Robin.
'No, that's my stick,' said Poo.
'How do you know that?'
'Cos yours has got one of my glass eyes attached to it.'

John Sissons

There Stands My Alfred, Majestic in His Finery, So Welcoming and With Such Warmth

"One hundred years old today," said mother and still taking centre stage. Body and shoulders squared, a knight in shining armour to his left and to his right. At his feet a red carpet. "Why was he called Alfred, Mother?" "Well!" said my mother, 'it's because he's Alfred the Grate.'

Zoë Nicholas

Memories

I stare at the little spring between my fingers. It's hard to believe it's been so long. So long, in fact, it's grown rusty with age.

I should rejoice in the memories of my childhood. Instead, I drown in them. Dreaming of simpler times when I believed everything lasted forever.

Connor Aedan

FROM ANOTHER ANGLE

How Do You Judge?

A film shows a woman on a road, a lorry is approaching
fast. A man appears to push her
into the lorry's path.
"How cruel!" You think.
In the next scene, the lorry has passed, and the woman is
safe in the man's arms.
He pulled, not pushed.
Don't judge!

John Williams

Happy Feet?

On our trip to New York, we wanted to bring something memorable back for our daughter. In Macy's we saw some trendy trainers.

"That will be great. It's the right size."

As she tried them on, she asked "Mum, do these look strange?"

The box contained two left footed trainers!

Angie Small

Hobbies

'Come in,' she said, dressed in her pink frilled apron she wore on Mondays.
I placed her six-year-old looking son's ball on the table.
'I'm sorry, he's always kicking it too high.' She blushed.
I leave smiling. Binoculars can only see through windows, but it was exactly how I imagined.

Hannah Esnouf

A Place for The Prized Portrait

"Right a bit… now up. No, the left side needs to go up. Perhaps it should be on the other wall. Yes, that one. That's good… over to the window a bit more. It's wonky.
Straighten it. Right side down. Perfect."
They stood back to admire their new picture.
Crash.

Angie Small

Majority Rules

That year, many more blind children were born.
Nobody knew why.
Freaks of nature, some said.
Next year, there were more.
Twenty years later millions marched, demanding a more unsighted-friendly world.
Fifty years on, most people cannot see.
The world is hard for us, the sighted minority.
Freaks, some say.

Terry Tyler

Together Forever

"Madam, wait!" She turned around.

"They're for you. They match your dress." She didn't understand anything.

"You've made me feel special. I want to spend my life with a woman like you." Beautiful words filled her ears. She didn't notice how her hands were cuffed with handcuffs matching her dress.

Olga

Bittersweet Pee

The forecourt was empty.

I filled the tank and paid.

As I returned to my car, I noticed a pool of green fluid
beside the front tyre.

Damn! My radiator's leaked.

I checked the puddle for the sweet taste of antifreeze.

A watchful Alsatian knew his pee would be bitter!

John Sissons

Power Of Attorney

'Too expensive,' was the mantra when Louise was young, and 'You're useless.' She hadn't passed that down to her own kids. Nor the beatings.

Now Mum keeps asking who Louise is. Matron wants to discuss unpaid bills, but she slips out. One way ticket to Mexico: sun, sea and freedom.

Karen Dures

Clumsy

I want to be a beauty queen.
Effortless and serene.
Done the salons, the shops, deportment lessons, the lot.
Frizzy hair in the rain, clumsily broken stilettos again.
Dress caught in the door, pants exposed, am competing no more.
I am a beauty queen,
At home, alone, just for me

Elizabeth Chandler

Science Project

"Time travel? Really?"

"Yeah."

To prove him wrong she spun the wheel, placed her palm on the reader.

"No!" Fear gripped him.

"Wow."

Relieved, he said, "See."

"But we're old."

“I've proven we can travel our own timeline. But if you travel to a time, you're not alive then—"

Heather Hartman

First Impressions

The bridegroom was wearing sunglasses, which annoyed the vicar.

'Do you have the rings?' he snapped.

'My best man does.'

'Where is he?'

'Here.'

The dog lay at his feet. His pouch bore the Guide Dogs logo, plus one embroidered word,

'Rings'.

'Sorry,' stumbled the vicar. 'Didn't see you there.'

Felicity Radcliffe

(Award Winner 2021)

LOVE STORIES?

A Traditional Love Story

Reaching for the last strand of pondweed, I tumble in.
Spluttering to the surface, I discover a frog squatting on my wrist.
"As tradition has it, if you kiss me, I'll turn into your handsome prince," he croaks.
Months later my prince and I marry and live happily ever after.

Ruth Bergman

Light In the Darkness

As dusk falls, I tremble before the flickering candle flame, lit in memory of Anthony.
I fear my heart will forever stutter with the jagged pain of losing him.
Ten years pass, and in a comforting annual ritual, the candle's steady glow brings forth fond memories and my enduring love.

Wendy Janes

Blind Date

War paint applied, thick lashes fluttering across the table.
He looks uncomfortable.
"They're just making finishing touches to the meal." She titters, flirting unashamedly. He's perfect.
A strange woman bursts in and sits next to him.
"Hi darling, sorry I'm late!"
The hosts enter, closely followed by some dishevelled idiot.

Nikki Rodwell

<u>First Love, Last Love</u>

She was my first date. She was my first love. She was my first wife
She was my only wife. She was the love of my life.
Now, after a lifetime together, she has gone, this love of my life.
A lifetime of memories, no longer a wife.
Last Love.

Graham Welton

Trygve The Trustworthy Dane Travels the Sea Sowing Wild Oats

Trygve sailed the longship to Anglia, homeland of his mother. He carried a cargo of furs and amber for trading with the Angles but he met Liv and found love so he stayed and they begat many children and a long line of Angles with a good dash of Viking.

Jo Whiffin

Love In a Time of Economic Crisis

Do you remember 1974? Three-day week, no leccy, we lit some candles, snuggled under a blanket. One thing led to another.

Fast forward to 2021. No petrol, can't afford the gas. We make love under a duvet now, slowly, to the sound of creaking joints. The joy is still there.

Debbie Collison

LIFECYCLE AND NATURE

Patience

I loved you from birth.
I nurtured you through the coldest winters.
I shaded you from the searing summer sun.
I talked to you daily.

At long last, today, my hard work rewarded,
you exploded with the most magnificent display.

Four years they said to see the beautiful magnolia flower.

Elizabeth Chandler

My Child

Your first wails subsided the moment you were placed in my arms.

You needed me.

Toddler to schoolboy, you challenged and enchanted in equal measure.

You learned more than I could ever teach.

Pride in my heart, a wistful smile on my lips, I watched you walk away into adulthood.

Wendy Janes

(Award Winner 2021)

Too Tidy?

It was a lovely walk: the sun beating down and the view improved by the newly pruned trees and trimmed verges. She remembered wincing, last year, when she had scuffed her shins on the unruly growth and fallen branches whilst picking blackberries. Oh wait… Where are all the blackberry bushes?

Angie Small

Fleeing The Nest Has Been in The Making Since the Very Day We Were Born

I'll give it another go today, said Paul. "Me too," said his brother, “but I can't help thinking of poor Humpty Dumpty's downfall, so here goes,” and off he went. My turn now thought Paul and flew off. “Come back Peter, come back Paul,” shouted Humpty Dumpty, “I'm all alone!”

Zoë Nicholas

My Grandson

How can it be?

Eighteen years have rushed on by
since our first new born grandchild
lay small and helpless in my arms.

I shared the joy of his first steps:
the highs and lows of childhood.

So soon that child became a man
who towers above his doting Nan.

Meg Brittain Clarke

Nature's Annual Winter to Spring Cycle

Once again, the seasonal battle commences:
Spring plants hold hard to their winter defences.
Cold bitter winds claw through the night:
Underground bulbs stay hidden from sight,
Until grows a weakness in winter's strong might.
Then young shoots encouraged reach for the light.
Again, flowering nature takes back the crown.

Meg Brittain Clarke

Hungry Muntjac Seen Early On A Winter's Morning, Bare Trees, Hardly Light, Quiescent Mist

Darkness slowly lifts, surroundings shrouded grey. Heavy frost white. This early, only birds moved. Then, silent as the mist, not even crunching on the frost, came the little muntjac, hungry but with a watchful eye. It was a matter of survival. He needed food but he needed to be wary.

Jo Whiffin

LESSONS FROM THE PAST

Don't Ignore the Locals

They warned me folk disappeared down the haunted caves.
I laughed, and went exploring.
When I emerged, the year was 1642.
They screamed; they thought I was a witch.
They burned me without trial.
I've haunted the caves for five hundred years.
To keep you away. To keep you safe.

Terry Tyler

On The Way Back from The Shops

The end of the lane: just fields
No cars. Our town, gone.
A passing shepherd told me the year: 1458.
Later, I died for Lancaster in the Wars of the Roses
My spirit drifts through centuries.
Now, in 2022, I watch my wife crying, wondering why I
never came home.

Terry Tyler

In Hindsight...

Beth sits down on the tram, mask tight over her face,
thinking about the last few years.
So much anger.
Violence.
Stupidity.
All so unnecessary...
The tram stops. Nearly home.
And now a pandemic! Even the Prime Minister caught it...
Still, at least he cares about us, that Lloyd George.

Jay Janes

A Journey from St Johns To Newtown On Newfoundland Went Badly Wrong

Every year Newfoundland residents visited Tobermory. Strong links followed the
Neptune II's experience - so nearly disaster, so nearly death for ten. No motor; no rudder; sails useless in the lengthy storm that entrapped them. The one day journey to Newtown ended on Mull forty-eight days later, providentially saving them.

Jo Whiffin

Ødger Guldbrandsen Successful Danish Invader of Monkwearmouth Jarrow Abbey In 794

Ødger Guldbrandsen, a strategist with wealth and weaponry, led the attack on the abbey. He was a magnificent leader, just, fair of face and formidably potent. Having successfully invaded, he travelled south through Northumbria and the Danelaw teaching the Norse ways and founding a Guldbrandsen dynasty which spread throughout Anglia.

Jo Whiffin

The Union Soldier's Wife: Fayette County, Pennsylvania. June 1865

I fed him, nursed his wounds, against my husband's wishes.
I swear I saw heaven in his eyes.
He said, 'Eighty years' time, we all be fighting together
'gainst some other imagined foe. We all just human beings.'
In the morning he was dead.
He still visits me, every day.

Terry Tyler

Searching For Treasure

Her father talked about it when she was a child.

Townsfolk rolled their eyes. Tall tales, they said. A myth. Somehow, during that time, she became obsessed with the possibility of its existence.

After his death, she searched. As she lay bleeding, she knew - happiness was just an urban legend.

Sarah Brentyn

Pawns in a Madman's Chess Game

He sets up the board, making careless moves.

First, he invades an innocent country; men fight, families weep. Then, the world watches as his madness unfolds with a childlike tantrum. He overturns the board and scatters the pieces to oblivion.

Mother enters, "Clear up this mess and get to bed!"

Nikki Rodwell

PANDEMIC

Masked Daylight Robbery

I was standing at the cashpoint outside of my bank.
Several smartly dressed city gents carrying briefcases and wearing blue surgical masks entered.
That wouldn't have happened before the pandemic, I thought.
Then they rushed out and ran off.
It was lucky that I'd drawn my money out in time.

John Sissons

Lockdown Losses

What did I miss during the lockdown, you ask?

Well, I yearned to meet my best friend in town, mooch about in clothes shops, share a pot of tea and a chat in our favourite cafe.

But above all, I missed my husband's smiling face taken from me by Covid.

John Sissons

How To Wear Your Hair in A Pandemic

Plait it round your ears like Carrie Fisher, or tie it in a ponytail to go with your comfiest jogging bottoms.
Don't bother washing it, unless you're appearing on zoom today.
Desperate for a pixie cut? Your home-schooled six-year-old will oblige, with a pair of blunt craft scissors.

Debbie Collison

November 2100

As Huntingdon Positive Thinkers' Group strolled along the promenade at Huntingdon On
Sea, Bardo turned to Abelia.
"I'm leaving the group. Sea levels still rising; days getting hotter and hotter; London under
water. Our world is finished."
Abelia thought hard. "Well at least all Covid restrictions have now been lifted."

David Seaton

Partygoers

Political partygoers Jim Lock and Bill Cove wobbled home having spent the evening
socialising at Down Steet Nightclub.
“So, which party are you voting for at the general election?” asked Jim. “Conservatives
maybe? Labour, Lib Dems, Green, not bothered?”
Bill burped and swayed. “I’ll just be voting for a party.”

David Seaton

MARKING LOSS

I Wanted Children So Badly

He didn't.
He said, 'Staying childfree means travel. Social life.
Freedom!'
When I was forty-five, he left me for a younger woman.
They now have two children.
He did want them, after all. Just not with me.

He gave her my life.
I have cats.

Terry Tyler

True Love and Being Instrumental to Him Was All I Ever Wanted

I lay nestled in his arms, against his heart being gently caressed, oh such sweet music we made. An unspoken love rarely apart. Over the years others came and went, but not me. Then one day I was discarded amongst the other instruments. I became the guitar that gently weeps.

Zoë Nicholas

Lonely Elizabeth

The black limousine rolls gently to a halt.
Sad and respectful, we watch the suited bodyguard open the door.
Standing alone and in grief, our dutiful Queen pauses to acknowledge the many mourners.
Hankies, once waved in jubilation, now soak up tears.
We yearn to cuddle our beloved great grandma.

John Sissons

Two Days Now, The Tides Rise and Fall

Impenetrable fog. The sea is invisible. He is out there, with Grandad, in a small kayak. Too small. The waters recede and I stand at the end of the lifeboat ramp. They give me strong, sweet tea but cannot look me in the eye. Hope slowly ebbs with the tide.

Simon Connor

The Silver Chain

Chosen with care for a special night. I shined bright in the moonlight. My master spun, giggled and we were happy. Shoved. Screamed. Yanked. My clasp broken. Thrown into a bag with nothing better than imposters. Displayed. Waiting for a new home. One that'll take me back to the moonlight.

Heather Hartmann

Undercover Assignment

I was to make him fall in love with me. Trust me.
To tell me the Group's secrets.
He found out; neither of us are of any further use.
I thought we would run together, but he has shunned me.
I wasn't lying, though.
I really did fall in love.

Terry Tyler

Flowers

The brightly colored carnations blur in my vision.

How is it fair that a little water sustains these flowers, but the very best medicine wasn't enough to save you?

I can't bear them anymore.

I grab the flowers and throw them out the door. They will not last the night.

Connor Aedan

The Truth

I killed my little sister.

An accident, they said.

A busy road, a momentary lapse;

Don't let it blight your life.

I never told them

About the whining, the pestering.

"I'm a big girl. I can cross by myself."

"Go on then," I said, and let go of her hand.

Yvonne Coppard

SEEKING RESPITE

The Vicious Cycle

A stubborn tap on his highchair tray.

A poisonous jab in his vein.

A journey begins through nightmare madness unknown to most.

A soft reprieve and a return to self brings hope.

A mother's sigh of relief.

The gorilla inside him awakens and raises his ugly head: the pain resumes.

Patricia Street

Divine Intervention

His inbox bulged with unread emails. The television blared. His smartphone pinged incessantly. He prayed for the world to stop.

A TV announcer interrupted the programme. Due to the energy crisis, an emergency power cut would begin in twenty minutes - duration unknown.

He thanked God for His rapid response.

Felicity Ratcliffe

The Everyday

Her case load includes
A rape victim,
A bereaved mother,
A suicidal teenager,
A traumatised mute child.
Another day of unrelenting misery.

Arriving home, her children are generous with their kisses,
Her husband's arms enfold her,
While dinner simmers on the stove.
Surrounded by their love,
She survives another day.

Yvonne Coppard

Neighbourhood Watch

The house opposite had been vacant for months.

I saw several sinister men enter.

Not new neighbours, I hoped.

Then a massive explosion threw me to the floor.

Their front door and windows were blown open.

No one came out.

I prayed for their souls and quieter neighbours next time.

John Sissons

My Old Friend

Depression pulls up over me like a thick, numbing dense duvet.
Muffling out sound and smells.
My old friend is back.
Soothingly talking into my ear
I succumb to it again.
My body welcomes the heaviness
Every ounce of energy flows out of my body, and I watch it go.

Keely McGuiness

Gravel Pit

Prom night. Liquor, beer, drugs, and sex. A teenage quarrel. "You f****r," she screams. He hits, she falls, striking her head.

I trudge an incline of quarried soil, crest the peak, and there, in a distant pool of still water bordered by tire tracks and footprints, a red dress floats.

Paul Rousseau

Its Flawless Ground Takes Me Below

I hear it as it drags me down to the fiery chambers
I watch on as I see it standing there, laughing at me, trying to destroy me
This thing does not want to be my friend.
It's intrusive thoughts; tackle me down waiting in the back of my mind.

Leanne Drain

Twins

There's always one pretty, one plain, Mum said.
Guess which one I was.
I trained hard, beat her on the track. Worked hard, made more money. Got a bigger house.
I even seduced her husband.
She's still the pretty one.
And the happy one.
She loves me. I hate her.

Terry Tyler

Mistaken Identity

His voice creeps down the stairs like a spider. Tries to ensnare me with its cadence, frightened and youthful.

He does not know who he is. Says he doesn't remember.

He lies.

The thing that used to be my son will remain locked up until one of us is dead.

Sarah Brentyn

(Award Winner 2021)

The Wolf at The Door

Dimming light eclipses his shadow outside.
"Bedtime!" I usher my brood from the conservatory to safety inside.
I'm woken by Ellie playing beside me, making red marks surface on her pasty thighs.
"Daddy says his handprints are on the walls, they will never fade."
Will we ever be safe again?

Nikki Rodwell

HEROES

The Mountain

He was coming down the mountain when the mist closed in.
He felt someone holding him back.
The clouds rose as quickly as they had descended.
He was standing on the edge of a precipice.
Wafting on the freshening breeze he caught the scent of his late wife's favourite perfume.

Sonia Kurta

Capt. Tom

For ninety-nine years I was just a man
Doing my best, doing what I can
I thought I'd lived and seen it all
Until one last time I heard the call
So I decided to do the walk, go round and round
One hundred times, nearly forty million pound.

Graham Welton

(Award Winner 2021)

<u>The Hit Man</u>

The hit man had a clear view as his target walked up the
path
to his front door.
It was essential he was annihilated before he divulged the
information.
He bent down to stroke his pet cat as the assassin squeezed
the trigger.
The bullet went harmlessly over his head.

Sonia Kurta

Stem Cell Regeneration

I went to the hospital
to get my bad hip mended.
I hoped an operation
would make my hip just splendid.
They took stem cells from my leg
then into my hip they went
and if they grow new cartilage,
it will be a miracle,
it will be heaven sent.

Jennifer Coville

Stolen Baby

She couldn't get the pram into the chemists.
The prescription was vital.
When she came out, the pram had disappeared.
Distraught, she heard a shout.
A man was hurrying towards her with the pram.
"That woman," he gasped, "She has Alzheimer's,
"I found her pushing your baby through the park."

Sonia Kurta

Intruders

The familiar woodland path, silence broken by crunching of paws, racing through frosty undergrowth.
A threat infiltrates my peaceful haven; a smell of burnt rope.
"Y'alright love?" A trio of hooded boys watching.
My pulse quickens.
The cavalry arrives, guarding like sentinels.
Backs of hoodies fade deep into the thicket

Nikki Rodwell

Retriever

Your desperate snout's a tragic periscope
Though you were bred to brave dark rivers,
this water's
monstrous mouth
brings black dismay.

But
a final sight has brought a sort of smile
to your exhausted muzzle.

The gasping child you dragged onto the shore,
Who'll caress her favored dog... no more.

Terry Kroenung

Comments from the Judges on the Winning Entries

First Place – Conjuring

The author has created a Brontesque dreamscape, with almost tangible atmosphere. We wonder what despicable, dark deed will facilitate a resurrection. Then we discover that there is no ghost, simply a leading lady who refuses to be written out. The saga is perfectly complete.

Second Place – The Flower

The clever wording within the imagery appears to stretch the story way beyond the fifty words. Is this because of the detail in the description, or down to the enormity of the consequences inferred? Although never actually mentioned, bees stayed in our minds long after reading this well-written modern fable.

Third Place - Happy

An intelligent, humorous take on a mashup of two classic children's stories. Great visualisation and a wicked punchline that made us laugh out loud.

Highly Commended – I Should Have Stayed at Home

Rock Star turned has-been? A saga that succinctly details the passage of time and changing circumstance, from youthful hope and expectation to disillusionment and middle age. We particularly enjoyed the wry humour of the concluding line.

The Editors

Georgia Rose

Georgia Rose is a writer and the author of the romantic and suspenseful Grayson Trilogy books: *A Single Step*, *Before the Dawn* and *Thicker than Water*, as well as the romantic thriller duology *Parallel Lies* and *Loving Vengeance*.

She has also started running workshops and providing one-to-one support for those wishing to learn how to independently publish and you can find her, under her real name, at www.threeshirespublishing.com.

Sally-Rose Runham

Sally-Rose has over 100 technical and refereed publications in environmental, rural and agricultural research. Sally-Rose began to hone her creative writing skills by joining Hunts Writers in 2015 and is now a committee member. An interest in green issues is maintained through St Ives eco-groups and wildlife trusts.

Our Judges…

… remain a mystery but we have uncovered some details about them, written in 50 words, naturally…

RAF - born into, dreamed of, achieved; before wings clipped by overwhelming mother love.
Positive problem solver who loves audiobooks on road trips, peace and quiet, family meals, horses (and mucking out), knitting, geraniums, bright crisp days and Middle Eastern food. Dislikes summer heat, dogs that jump up and chillies.

And, introducing our new judge…

A lover of words; their root, their meaning and the sound they make. I enjoy reading stories and also listening to them in all forms. I love the tradition of telling stories as songs and ballads. I love word play in all its forms. Stories make the world go round.

Acknowledgements

Georgia Rose and Sally-Rose Runham would like to thank all the authors who entered this competition. We appreciate your support and hope to hear from you again in the future. We also thank our wonderful judges for their time and diligence.

Lastly, we thank Simon Emery for his superb cover design for all of our anthologies.

Rating and Review Request

Thank you for reading. If you are able to rate this book or leave a few words as a review, it would be much appreciated.

You are invited to enter the Roses Mini Saga Competition 2023.

What is a mini saga?

A mini saga is a fun way to tell a story in 50 words exactly, with a title of no more than 16 words.

It should have a beginning, a middle and an end, and some period of time should pass through the story.

*****

The Guidelines and Rules

Any theme is accepted and the number of entries is unlimited. The fee is £2 per entry. Members of the following writing groups, Huntingdon Writers, Mendlesham Writers and Needingworth Scribblers are permitted three free entries each in 2023 due to their support with the launch of the competition.

The deadline day for all submissions is by 11.59 pm on 28 February 2023 and all other details can be found at:

https://rosesminisagacompetition.wordpress.com

Any entries found not to comply with the rules will be returned for further editing and resubmission.

Hyphenated words – try to avoid them, but, if essential, they will only be accepted if they are in the Oxford English Dictionary.

There will be at least one independent judge and all entries will be anonymously sent to them.

Mini sagas previously entered, and even awarded prizes, in other competitions may be entered and revised entries as referred to in the judge's comment section above may also be entered.

Entries should be written in English.

Prizes

£75 first prize, £50 second prize, £25 third prize and a new £15 prize for highly commended.

Prizes provided by Cambridge Projects (hereinafter called the 'Publisher').

Award Announcement

The Awards will be announced by email on 30 April 2023.

Publication

The winning entries and any other entries chosen at the discretion of the Publisher will be included in an anthology of mini sagas which will be available to buy from Amazon as either an eBook or paperback by the 1 July 2023. Copyright for each mini-saga will remain with the author.

Email Addresses

All email addresses for submissions made will be added to a mailing list at Mailchimp for the purposes of keeping entrants informed about anything to do with the competition, including the announcement of awards.

Entrants will have the opportunity to unsubscribe from this mailing list at any time and the email addresses will not be passed on to any third party.

Printed in Great Britain
by Amazon

11237254R00062